MOG
and the V. E. T.

written and illustrated by
Judith Kerr

HarperCollins *Children's Books*

For Susannah Thraves

Other books by Judith Kerr include:

The Tiger Who Came to Tea*

Mog the Forgetful Cat*

Mog's Christmas*

Mog and the Baby*

Mog in the Dark

Mog's Amazing Birthday Caper

Mog and Bunny

Mog and Barnaby

Mog on Fox Night

Mog and the Granny

Mog's Bad Thing

Goodbye Mog

When Willy Went to the Wedding

How Mrs Monkey Missed the Ark

Birdie Halleluyah!

The Other Goose

Twinkles, Arthur and Puss*

Goose in a Hole

One Night in the Zoo*

My Henry

The Great Granny Gang*

The Crocodile Under the Bed

Mog's Christmas Calamity

*also available on audio CD

First published in hardback in Great Britain by William Collins Sons & Co Ltd in 1996. First published in paperback by Picture Lions in 1997. This edition published by HarperCollins Children's Books in 2005

39

ISBN-13: 978-0-00-717128-6

Visit our website at: www.harpercollins.co.uk

Printed and bound in China

One day Mog was trying to catch a butterfly.
She jumped high in the air. She jumped and jumped.
Suddenly something happened to her paw.
It was very sore.

She smelled it. It was still sore.

Then she licked it, but it was still sore.

She tried to walk on it, but it was very, very sore.

Mog thought, "I've got three other paws.
I'll just walk on them instead."

"What's the matter with Mog?" said Nicky.
Debbie said, "I think she's got a sore paw."
"Poor Mog," said Mr Thomas. "Let me see."
But Mog wouldn't let anyone see her paw.
It was too sore.

"Oh dear," said Mrs Thomas. "If it's no better tomorrow she'll have to go to the vee ee tee." She said vee ee tee instead of vet so that Mog wouldn't understand.
Mog hated going to the vet, but Mrs Thomas thought she probably couldn't spell.

That evening Mog did not want to eat
her supper because her paw was too sore.
It was so sore that she couldn't sleep.

In the morning, she did not eat her breakfast.
She just lay on the floor feeling sad.

Suddenly she was not on the floor anymore.
Mrs Thomas had picked her up.
Mog thought, "What's happening? It's rude
to pick me up without asking me first."

Then she was in a basket.
But it was not her proper basket.
It was a nasty basket that shut her in.
Mog did not like that basket.
She meowed a big meow.

Debbie said, "It's all right, Mog.
We're taking you to have your paw made better."
But Mog just wanted to get out of the basket.

Then they were in the car. It made a big noise and all the houses and trees and people rushed past outside. Mog knew that was not right. She meowed and meowed.

At last the houses stopped rushing past and suddenly Mog was in a room.

Waiting Room

It was a room with lots of other animals.
Mog thought, "I knew it! I knew it! This is the
place I hate!" And she meowed more than ever.

The other animals were
sitting quietly with their people.
They were surprised to hear Mog
make so much noise.

"It's all right, Mog," said Debbie.
"It's all right, Mog," said Nicky.
"It's all right, puss," said the nurse.
But Mog wouldn't stop meowing.
After a while the other animals thought
perhaps Mog knew something they didn't.

The dogs began to bark.

The parrot began to squawk.

Even the hamster
said "Eek! Eek!"

They made so much noise
that the vet came to see
what was happening.
"Oh, it's Mog," said the vet.
"I thought it might be.
Perhaps I'd better see her first."

Mog suddenly thought she liked the shut-in basket after all.
The vet tried to look at her, but it was very difficult.

"Perhaps this way will be easier," said the vet.

"There," said the vet at last.
"Now, let's have a look at that paw."

He did something very quickly.
Then he said, "All done.
She had a nasty thorn in her paw,
and look – here it is!"

"Now I'll just give her a little pill and…

…Ow!" said the vet.
"Oh Mog!" said Debbie.
"I'm so sorry," said Mrs Thomas.
"Watch out for that cat!"
shouted the vet.
"Quick! Catch it!" shouted
the nurse.

"I'll catch it,"
thought a big dog.
"And I'll catch it too,"
thought a little dog.
"But I'll catch it first,"
thought a third dog.

"Heel!" "Sit!" "Stay!" "Come back!"
shouted the dogs' people.
But the dogs took no notice.

"They're all going wild!" shouted the nurse.
The hamster got mixed up in the wild rush.
The vet got mixed up in it too.

"Stop! We can't have animals going wild," said the vet.
The dogs' people all shouted, "Heel!" "Sit!" "Stay!" and
"Come back!" again and after a while the dogs stopped.

"Come on, Mog," said Nicky. "You're a very silly cat."
"Back into your basket," said Debbie.

"Goodbye," said the vet. "I think she'll be all better
in the morning after a good night's sleep."

And that night Mog did have a good sleep.

But the vet did not have
a good sleep.

The vet had a dream. It was a dream about wild animals.

Mog had a dream too, but it was a lovely dream.
Mog dreamt that she was a butterfly.

And in the morning her paw was no longer sore.
It was not sore when she licked it.
It was not sore when she walked on it.
It was not sore when she jumped up high.
She was better. She was all better.
She was totally, completely better.

And the vet was almost better too.